PEDRO PENGUIN
Let's Go To The Beach
Vamos a la Playa

T.Fielding-Lowe Company, LLC., Publisher
www.tfieldinglowecompany.com

This book belongs to / Este libro pertenece a

_____

We dedicate this book first and foremost to Papi Penguin (Pedro Saquic Chavajay).
Thank you for your endless love and support. You have believed in us always and without you this book would not have been created. The bond you share as father and son is unbreakable. You are the best!!
We love you so much, so much!!

We would also like to thank Ms Shannon. One of Pedro Samuel's Head Start teachers for being the inspiration behind Shannon shark. Thank you for sharing such a memorable moment with our little Penguin. We will never forget his time with you, Ms. Tracy and Ms Joann.

Special thanks to everyone at Children's Friend who was an inspiration to Pedro Samuel in one way or another. Thanks to this valuable experience Pedro is more than ready for Big Boy School.   You will be missed as Pedro Penguin begins a new chapter.

Love and Hugs

Dedicamos este libro primeramente a Papi Pingino (Pedro Saquic Chavajay).
Gracias por tu amor y apoyo sin fin. Siempre has creido en nosotros y sin ti este libro no seria creado.
El vinculo que comparten como Padre y hijo es inquebrantable. Eres el mejor!!
Te amamos demas, demas.

Queremos tambien agradecer a Ms Shannon una de las maestras de Pedro Samuel en Head Start. Por ser la inspiracion detras de Shannon Shark la tiburona. Gracias por compartir un momento tan inolvidable con nuestro pequeno Pingino. Nunca olvidaremos el tiempo compartido contigo, Ms Tracy y Ms Joann.

Agradecemos en especial a todos en Children's Friend que han sido de inspiracion a Pedro Samuel de una manera o otra. Gracias a esta experiencia tan valiosa Pedro esta mas que listo para la escuela de ninos grandes. Les extranaremos mientras Pedro Pingüino comienza un nuevo capitulo.

Amor u Abrazos

It is a beautiful day!
Get on your feet.
We are going on a trip to the beach.

Es un hermoso día!
Ponte de pie.
Vamos a ir de viaje a la playa.

Lunch is packed
with all kinds of fruit.
At the beach,
I will share with you too!

Almuerzo listo
con frutas.
Vamos a la playa,
contigo también compartiré!

The warm sun,
crashing waves,
what a way to spend our day!

El cálido sol,
las olas rompiendo.
¡Qué manera de pasar el día!

At the beach,
we run and play.
Oh! I am having fun today!

En la playa,
corremos y jugamos.
Oh! Como me divierto hoy!

As we swim in the waves,
who do we see?
Shannon Shark swimming to me.

Mientras nadamos en las olas.
¿A quién vemos venir?
Tiburóna Shannon nadando a mí.

"Hello Shannon!"
"What wonderful waves!"
"Let's enjoy this beautiful day."

"Hola Shannon!"
"Que maravillosas olas!"
"Disfrutemos de este hermoso día."

"I'm one grumpy shark."

"Don't you see?"

"I just can't find anything to eat."

"Soy una tiburóna gruñóna."

"No puedes ver?"

"No encuentro nada para comer."

"Don't do that!"
"I know just what to do."
"I love to share
my food with you."

"No hagas eso!"
"Ya se lo que hare."
"Me encanta compartir
mi comida contigo."

Not a moment too soon.
A fruit salad was made
for me and you.

Sin un momento que perder.
Se preparó una ensalada de
frutas para ti y para mi.

Let's say thanks,
for this food.
Grateful hearts are now due.

Demos gracias.
por la comida.
Con corazónes agradecidos.

Pedro Penguin Favorite Fruit Salad
Ensalada de frutas favorita de Pedro Pingüino

1 cup strawberries / Una taza de frezas

1 cup watermelon / Una taza de sandia

4 mandarin oranges / 4 mandarinas

2 bananas / 2 bananos

4 kiwis / 4 kiwis

6 Oz blueberries / 6 onzas de arandanos

6 Oz seedless grapes / 6 onzas de uvas sin semillas

For dressing mix / Para aderezo mezcla

1/4 cup honey / 1/4 taza de miel

2 tbsp fresh lime juice / 2 cucharadas de jugo de Limon Verde

Mix fruit salad with dressing and enjoy with family.

Mezclar ensalada de frutas con aderezo y disfrute en familia.

Momma and Pappa Penguin

Mami y Papi Pinguino

About the Authors

Pedro Samuel Saquic and Ana Echevarria De Saquic are a mother/son duo who struggled to stay positive in the face of this new challenge called COVID19. So when young Pedro told the sweet story of a Penguin and a Shark becoming unlikely friends, an idea was born -why not turn this story into a book as a family project? This fun endeavor pulled them closer as a family and raised their spirits.

Ana and Pedro live in Rhode Island. Ana enjoys writing and crafts while Pedro loves watching gaming videos and playing his Nintendo Switch games. They're tight-knit and enjoy spending family time at the beach. Pedro is an energetic young one who enjoys nature and playing in the great outdoors. The pair hopes to inspire other families to try new activities and stay positive no matter what obstacles arise in life.

Pedro Samuel Saquic y Ana Echevarria De Saquic son un duo de Madre e hijo quienes lucharon para maintenance positivos en medio del nuevo reto llamado COVID19. Asi que cuando el pequeño Pedro conto la tierna historia de un Pingüino y una tiburóna que se convierten en amigos improbable, nacio una idea- porque no convertir esta historia en un libro como projecto de familia? Esto uñio a la familia y levanto sus animos.

Ana y Pedro viven en Rhode Island. Ana disfruta escribir y hacer manualidades mientras a Pedro le encanta ver videos y jugar sus video juegos en su Nintendo Switch. Son muy unidos y les gusta pasar tiempo de familia en la playa. Pedro es un niño energetico el cual disfruta de la naturaleza y jugar afuera Ambos desean inspirar a otras familias a probar nuevas actividades y mantenerse positivas no importando los obstaculos de la vida.

CPSIA information can be obtained
at www.ICGtesting.com
Printed in the USA
BVHW061551291021
619893BV00001B/8